Mindfulness
A Superpower

Jill McDougall

Contents

What Is Mindfulness?

Mindfulness is a powerful way to bring more peace and enjoyment into your life. It is practised by millions of people around the world and is not difficult to learn. Mindfulness activities don't require any special equipment, and they can take as little as ten minutes a day to do.

So, what is mindfulness? Simply put, it is the act of paying attention to just one thing. One Australian school student described it as "putting your mind in one place". An example of a mindfulness activity is slowly counting your breaths, in and out. By concentrating on just one thing, we clear our mind of other thoughts and worries. In this way, we become mindful rather than having a mind that is full!

You can practise mindfulness on your own or with friends.

By paying attention to just one thing, like your breath, we can move from a mind that is full to a more relaxed, mindful headspace.

Buddhist monks practise mindfulness through **meditation** in Chiang Mai, Thailand.

Origins of Mindfulness

The concept of mindfulness can be traced back to the word *sati*, which comes from the ancient Pāli (pronounced *pah-lee*) language of northern India. Basically, *sati* means awareness, or paying attention.

For thousands of years, mindfulness has been an important part of many religions. Buddhist monks and nuns practised mindfulness more than 2000 years ago, and they continue to practise it today. In the Islamic religion, mindfulness is practised by paying great attention to one's actions, thoughts and feelings. Mindfulness is also a part of the Christian tradition through meditation and prayer.

An American scientist, Dr Jon Kabat-Zinn, was one of the first people in the **Western world** to use mindfulness as a way of helping people who were troubled. In 1979, he founded the Center for Mindfulness in Massachusetts, USA. Dr Kabat-Zinn's mindfulness program was used in hospitals to help patients who were suffering from pain and **anxiety**.

In recent times, people all around the world have begun to practise mindfulness because they find it helpful in their daily lives. This has led scientists to study how mindfulness works and how it affects the brain.

Some schools have programs for students to practise mindfulness.

Mindfulness Under the Microscope

Scientists have conducted many studies to investigate the effects of mindfulness. Most of the **research** shows that when mindfulness exercises are practised on a regular basis, people can experience some amazing benefits.

Mindfulness training has been found to reduce **stress** and anxiety, and boost **self-esteem**. It can also help people feel more kindly towards themselves and others. Mindfulness has even been found to improve the performance of athletes.

One exciting finding is that our memory improves when we regularly do mindfulness activities. Another result is that we can concentrate for longer on tasks. Therefore, mindful people make better learners!

Mindfulness can help with any skill that requires concentration and calmness, like performing music.

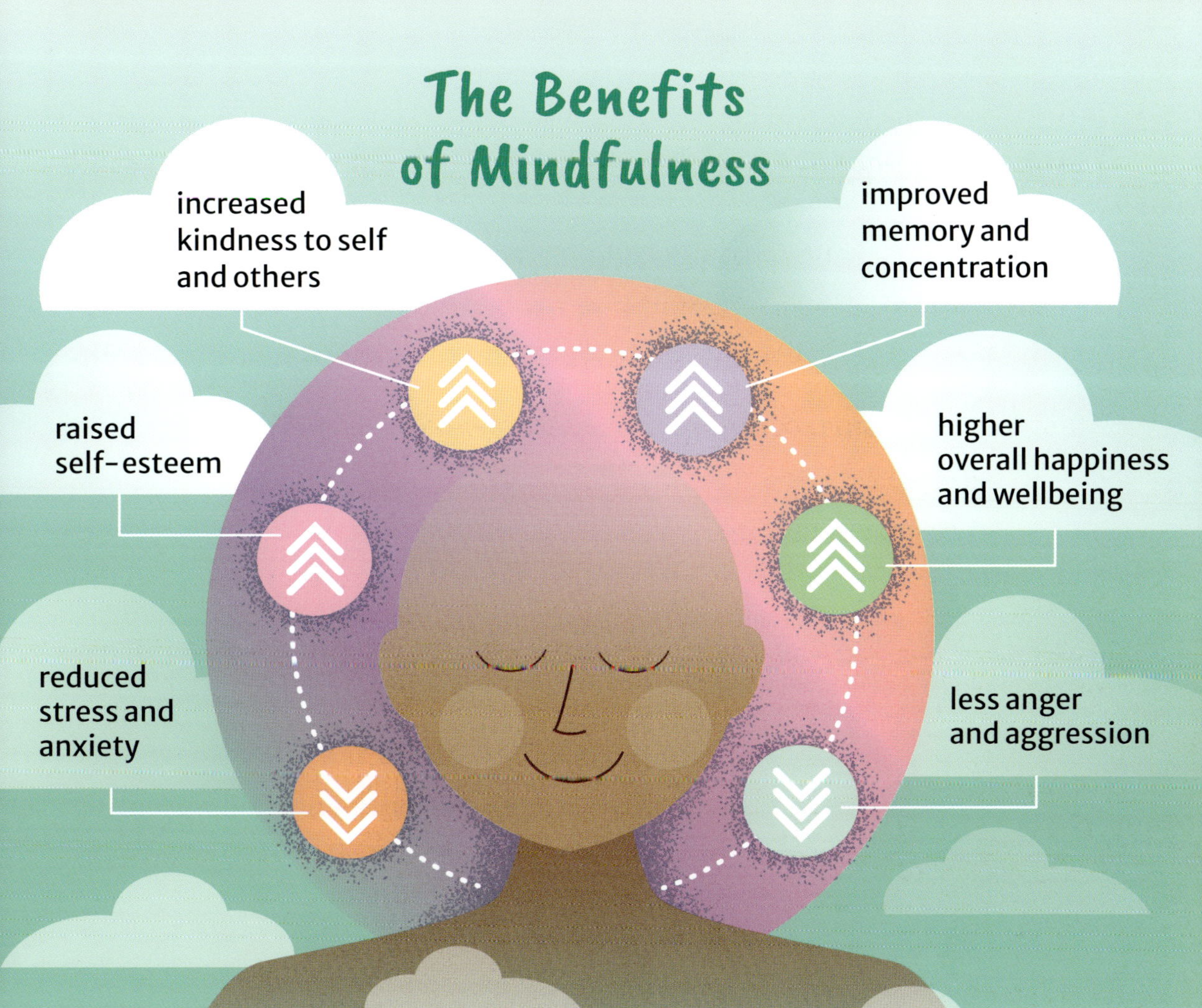

There is such a range of benefits to mindfulness that many schools around the world have introduced mindfulness activities in the classroom. These schools have seen some pleasing results, such as calmer, happier students and fewer behavioural issues.

When you consider all the benefits of mindfulness, it's no wonder some people call it a superpower.

The Amazing Benefits of Mindfulness

When you practise mindfulness, you develop skills to help you deal with difficult situations. For example, you learn how to take a few deep, mindful breaths and stay in the present moment. When you calm down in this way, you feel more relaxed and are able to make better decisions.

Mindfulness helps people to calmly ride the waves of their thoughts and acknowledge their emotions without feeling overwhelmed by them.

Young people who practise mindfulness say that it helps them relax in all sorts of situations. A fifteen-year-old boy who did an eight-week course in mindfulness found that it helped him feel calmer. He had suffered from constant anxiety and felt stressed at home, at school and even when he was out with friends. He said, "Mindfulness helps me chill out and clear my head."

How can mindfulness training have such a positive impact on our emotions? Dr Kabat-Zinn teaches people that emotions are like waves in the ocean. We can't escape from the waves but, through mindfulness, we find the strength and **wisdom** inside ourselves to calmly accept the waves and ride them. Dr Kabat-Zinn says, "You can't stop the waves, but you can learn to surf!"

One researcher used mindfulness training to help a group of ten-year-old children manage their **aggressive** behaviour. The children were taught to count ten breaths to calm themselves down when they began to feel upset or angry. By pausing to count their breaths, the children were able to see the issue that was troubling them more clearly and then work things out in a calm way. A year later, many of the children were still using this technique on their own.

People can practise mindfulness in any quiet spot.

Another benefit of mindfulness is called "self-compassion". This means that we treat ourselves with the same kindness and care that we would give to a good friend. Self-compassion is a wonderful gift to ourselves, and it comes when we practise mindfulness on a regular basis.

Social media can be one cause of self-criticism, especially for young people. When we look at unrealistic photos on the internet, we compare ourselves to the "perfect" people we see. This can lead to lots of negative feelings, such as self-loathing. However, by practising mindfulness and self-compassion, we learn to accept ourselves just as we are. Mindfulness helps us to be kinder and gentler to ourselves.

Photos on social media often show only the most perfect versions of people.

Mindfulness training also helps us to act more kindly towards others, no matter how old we are. An eight-year-old boy who was taught mindfulness at school said, "When I settled my mind, I felt my kindness getting bigger and bigger. It was even bigger than me."

An older student found that practising mindfulness helped her to become a better friend. She said that instead of getting annoyed with one of her friends, she was able to stop feeling "full of judgements" and concentrate on the things about her friend that she liked.

Acting with kindness towards others has a positive impact on people's relationships.

Many celebrities practise mindfulness to help them cope with their busy lives. The US singer Ariana Grande regularly practises meditation, which is a form of mindfulness. She says that meditation helps her keep calm while she juggles her busy schedule of recording music and making videos and performing in concerts.

Ariana Grande performs onstage during her Sweetener world tour in 2019.

Training the Brain

Mindfulness is such a powerful technique that it changes the structure of the human brain. It not only changes the shape of the brain, but it also changes how the brain works. This is because the brain is a muscle that responds to mental exercise in the same way that our bodies respond to physical exercise. So, we have the power to train our brains!

A group of scientists at Harvard University in Massachusetts, USA, found that when people practised mindfulness for eight weeks, one part of their brain, called the hippocampus, grew bigger and stronger. This is an important finding, especially for students, because the hippocampus helps with learning and memory.

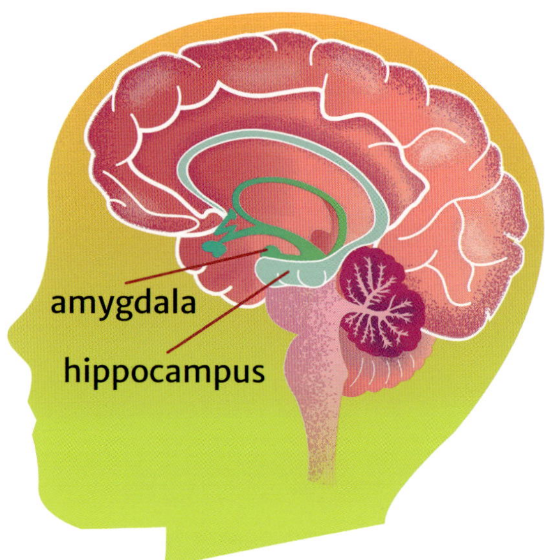

The size of the hippocampus and amygdala in the human brain can be changed by practising mindfulness.

The scientists also found that another part of the brain, the amygdala (pronounced *ah-MIG-de-la*), grew smaller. The amygdala is responsible for negative feelings, such as fear and anxiety. It is not surprising, then, that the people who took part in this study reported that they felt a greater sense of **well-being**.

It is clear that mindfulness practice not only helps us become better learners, but it can also change the way we think, feel and act.

Using mindfulness, we can actively train our brains, unravel messy thoughts and increase our well-being.

Kevin Durant plays in an NBA basketball game for the Golden State Warriors in 2019.

Many top athletes use mindfulness exercises to train their brains to achieve greater sporting results.

In the USA, the Golden State Warriors basketball team in San Francisco uses mindfulness to improve their performance. After they won the NBA (National Basketball Association) championship, team member Kevin Durant said, "I just tried to stay in the moment the whole series, and I think that worked for me".

Caroline Buchanan is an Australian world champion BMX and mountain bike rider who also practises mindfulness. Buchanan's sport is potentially dangerous, and she must remain focused while hurtling around the track at top speed. Buchanan says that being mindful helps her stay calm under pressure.

Caroline Buchanan competes in the elite women's quarter finals at BMX Supercross in 2015.

Mindfulness in Schools

Teachers around the world have found that mindfulness activities help students feel more settled and happy at school. They say it calms the whole classroom. Mindfulness has a positive effect on concentration, creativity, self-confidence and **compassion**.

In some schools, mindfulness is seen as an essential life skill and is an important part of the curriculum.

Yoga is a mindful activity that can also be good for physical fitness.

At a primary school in Canada, twenty students in a year one class practised mindfulness two times a week for six weeks. When they were asked to describe how they felt about the activities, the words they used most often were "fun", "enjoy", "great" and "happy". Some older students said they would use mindfulness breathing when they were fighting with a sibling or when they were feeling angry. Others used the strategies in times of difficulty, such as when they were in hospital or at the dentist.

A student who completed a mindfulness course at a school in Singapore said:

"The Moving Mindfully course really helped me, because I am an active person (dance and athletics), and it has helped me get over stage fright and perform better."

Mindfulness can help students with social issues, such as bullying. At a number of schools in the USA where bullying was a problem, the bullying behaviour reduced by 50 per cent after mindfulness training. The people who engaged in bullying behaviour were able to control their emotions better, and the students who were being bullied felt stronger about standing up for themselves.

A teacher who helped lead the program said, "When the students are more aware of their thoughts and feelings, they can choose how to react and behave."

Feeling in control of reactions and behaviour can help people work with others more easily.

Another benefit of mindfulness programs in schools is the impact they have on students' confidence. Teachers in the schools', mindfulness programs in the USA had noticed that when year eight students participated in group tasks, they were reluctant to make suggestions for fear of being judged by their classmates. After mindfulness training, the students were more willing to speak up and were less worried about the opinions of others. As a result, the groups became more creative and better at problem solving.

Some schools use mindfulness **apps** to guide their program. In this way, teachers and students can practise mindfulness together. The apps include **guided meditations**, mindful games, soothing sounds and inspiring videos.

Listening to soothing sounds or relaxing music is one way to practise mindfulness.

Having a Superpower

Mindfulness can help people better support themselves and their friends.

Mindfulness training can achieve excellent results for our minds and bodies. It helps us to feel better, stay in the present moment, be kind and make good decisions. Training programs in schools have lasting benefits, both inside school and out. In fact, mindfulness is a skill that everyone can use throughout their lives. Learning how to be mindful really is like having a superpower. By tapping into your inner strength, you become your own superhero – no matter what life throws your way!

Are you ready? It's time to take a deep breath and try it ...

Mindfulness can be a superpower, helping people to feel more confident and calm.

Simple Mindfulness Exercises

Sound Focus

Materials

- a timer
- a quiet place

Steps

1. Set the timer for ten minutes.
2. Sit in a quiet place with your eyes closed.
3. Take deep, slow breaths, in and out.

4. Listen for any sounds you can hear nearby, placing all your attention on one sound at a time.
5. If your mind wanders, gently bring your thoughts back to the sound.
6. Listen for sounds that are further away, moving from one sound to the next.
7. After ten minutes, slowly open your eyes.

Notice if your mind and body feel more relaxed and calm.

Body Squeeze

Materials

- a quiet place

Steps

1. Lie on your back in a quiet place and close your eyes.
2. Squeeze the muscles in your legs and feet as tightly as you can.
3. Relax the muscles and take three slow breaths.
4. Now, squeeze the muscles in your arms and hands as tightly as you can.
5. Relax the muscles and take three slow breaths.
6. Now, squeeze all the muscles in your face. Don't forget your eyes.
7. Relax all the muscles in your body and take three slow breaths.

Notice if your mind and body feel more relaxed and calm.

Mindful Eating

Materials

- a small piece of food, such as a grape or almond

Steps

1. Hold the food to your nose and breathe in its scent. How does it smell?
2. Close your eyes and explore the food through touch. What does it feel like? Is it hard or soft? Grainy or sticky? Moist or dry?
3. Open your eyes and look carefully at the food. Notice its shape and all of its colours. Notice its texture. Is it smooth or bumpy?

4. Take a small bite and chew very slowly. Notice how the food feels in your mouth. Notice the muscles you use to chew.
5. Notice if the flavour changes, moment to moment.
6. Take about 20 more seconds to very slowly finish your first bite of food. Be aware of the sensations of chewing and tasting.
7. Now, take your second and last bite.
8. Chew very slowly and pay attention, moment to moment. Notice the sensations and movements of chewing and the sensation of swallowing.

Notice if your mind and body feel more relaxed and calm.

Colour Your Breath

Materials

- a marker pen
- coloured pencils
- an A4 sheet of paper

Steps

1. Take a deep breath and pick up the marker pen. Then, starting in the middle of the paper, draw a line as you breathe out.
2. Without lifting the pen, draw another line as you breathe in. The line can go in any direction.
3. Continue drawing a line with each breath, without lifting the pen.
4. Keep going as you breathe in and out, counting your breaths.
5. After 30 breath cycles, put down the pen.
6. Use the coloured pencils to decorate the shapes you have made.

Glossary

aggressive angry or violent

anxiety a mental health condition that causes fear or worry

apps applications, or programs, that are downloaded to a device

Buddhist following the religion of Buddhism

compassion a feeling of sympathy and concern for someone

guided meditations mindfulness activities that are led by another person

meditation a practice used to focus the mind

research scientific information, sometimes found by doing experiments

self-esteem confidence in your own worth or abilities

stress a feeling of strain from mental or emotional pressure

well-being the state of being comfortable, healthy or happy

Western world the group of countries with populations of mainly European ancestry

wisdom experience and knowledge

Index